EMERGENCY!

by Lisa Norby

illustrated by Paul Gibbs

Table of Contents

Chapter 1 Fluffy the Alligator

Susan and Emma's parents were packing the car for an overnight trip. "I'm sorry we can't take you kids along this time," their mother told them. "I'm sure you'll be fine with Aunt Claire. At least I think you will."

"Don't be silly," said their father. "Your sister is highly capable. What could go wrong?"

Before anyone could answer his question, Aunt Claire's car turned into the driveway. She scrambled out. "I hope I'm not late," she said. "I had some important business downtown, and I just lost track of the time."

"You could try wearing a watch," her sister said.

Aunt Claire waved her arms. Silver bracelets jangled on both wrists. "Watches are so dull and practical," she said. "I prefer fun things."

Aunt Claire was the owner of a store called The Junque Shoppe. That was a fancy way of saying that she sold junk. Some of the things in the store were antiques, but others were just old.

Aunt Claire did give good presents, though.

This time she had a pretty box filled with old beads for Susan. For four-year-old Emma she had a stuffed alligator.

The minute Emma saw the alligator she forgot all about saying goodbye to her mom and dad. "Fluffy can sit on my bed," she announced.

"Fluffy isn't a good name for an alligator," Susan said.

"Don't upset your sister," her mom warned.

Susan rolled her eyes. She was just trying to be helpful.

Mom and dad finally said their goodbyes and left. After dinner, Emma sat down to watch a video about dinosaurs. Susan looked at her beads.

"Let's make some popcorn," said Aunt Claire.

Susan got out the popcorn box. Her aunt started cutting open one package and pouring it into a pan.

"No!" Susan yelped. "Not like that! You put the whole package in the microwave."

"How about that!" said Aunt Claire. "I don't have these fancy appliances in my kitchen. I guess I just don't understand them."

Chapter 2 The Flood

Aunt Claire might be impractical in some ways. But when it came to real food, she knew how to cook. The next morning, she made delicious blueberry pancakes for breakfast. She even showed Emma how to decorate them with smiley faces made of blueberries and bananas.

Susan had soccer practice that afternoon. When breakfast was over she decided to collect her things. Her socks were still in the dryer. But when she started down the steps to the basement she got a big surprise.

Water poured from a leaky pipe in the corner. The floor was flooded. The water was two inches deep and rising fast.

She rushed back to the kitchen to warn her aunt. "I think we have a problem," Susan said.

At first, Aunt Claire was calm. She sat down at the kitchen table and started calling plumbers. But it was Sunday morning. No one was at work. Some of the plumbers had answering machines, and Aunt Claire left the same message for all of them. "Please call back. It's an emergency. We have a flood here."

Susan tried to figure out what her mother would do. "Maybe there's a way to turn the water off," she said. "I think mom did it once when the construction workers were adding the extra bathroom."

"I'll go check," Aunt Claire said. "But if you're going to come with me, put your rain boots on. There's no telling what's floating around down there."

Emma was listening in the doorway. Her eyes grew wide. "Are there alligators down there?" she asked. She looked hopeful.

"No," Susan told her. "Fluffy is the only alligator in this house." She pulled on her boots to make her aunt happy.

When she got to the basement, Aunt Claire was peering behind the washing machine. There was a maze of pipes. Each of them had a turn-off valve. Aunt Claire tried them all. But water continued to pour from the leaky pipe in the corner.

Chapter 3 The Firefighters

Along the far wall of the basement were shelves stuffed with old books, tools, and boxes of winter clothes. "Those plumbers won't call back for hours," Aunt Claire said. "By then, everything will be ruined. I'm going to call the firehouse. Someone there will know what to do."

Aunt Claire ran back up the stairs. Susan stayed behind. She was sure there was another valve somewhere. She could hear her aunt up in the kitchen, talking on the phone. "I have an emergency here. There are two children in the house," she heard her aunt saying. "The whole place is filling up." Her aunt sounded frantic.

Emma was in the kitchen too. She was running around, shrieking, "Alligator! Alligator!"

Susan wanted to figure out this water problem. The water level was rising. Suddenly, she had an idea. There was a closet next to the laundry room where her parents kept old toys and sports equipment. She looked inside and saw the water meter. Underneath it was a large valve. That was where her mom had shut off the water.

She turned the valve. The water spewing from the pipe slowed to a trickle. Then it stopped. Susan took a deep breath and relaxed.

At that moment, Susan heard a siren outside the house. She went upstairs. Two firefighters were at the front door. "Is everyone here all right?" the taller one asked.

"It's over," Susan told them showing them into the house. "The basement was flooding. But I figured out how to turn the water off."

Aunt Claire looked embarrassed. "I'm sorry for bothering you guys. I guess I got too excited."

"We volunteer firefighters respond to all kinds of emergencies," the tall man said. "But next time you might try asking one of your neighbors for help first."

"Actually, we were curious," the other firefighter said. "We've never had an alligator emergency before."

"Fluffy," said Emma. "His name is Fluffy."

"Okay," said the men in unison.

Aunt Claire waved her hands. "I wish there was something I could do to make it up to you."

"We're having a pancake breakfast next Saturday to raise money for a new fire truck," he said. "We sure could use another griddle cook."

That was how Aunt Claire became a cook for the volunteer firefighters' pancake breakfast. Susan helped out in the kitchen too.

They made the best pancakes ever with apples, blueberries, and bananas. They had syrup, butter, jam and powdered sugar to top off the pancakes.

One of the firefighters came to the griddle and showed off by flipping some pancakes in the air and catching them on a plate. He bowed to his clapping audience.

Afterwards, the firefighters gave Susan a tour. She saw the beds where the firefighters slept. She saw the dummy that they used to teach CPR. She slid down the firefighter's pole, and even got to sit in the driver's seat of the fire truck. She pictured herself becoming a volunteer firefighter some day. She'd be ready for any emergency, including a flood in a basement.

Comprehension Check

Summarize

Use a Theme Map to record clues and the theme, or main idea, of the story. Then use the chart to summarize the story.

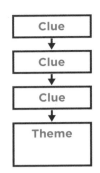

Think and Compare

1. Reread page 12. What is the main idea of this page? *(Analyze Theme)*

2. What steps can you take if you have an emergency in your home? To whom should you go for help? *(Apply)*

3. Many towns have volunteer firefighters. Volunteers do not get paid. Why is volunteer work important? *(Evaluate)*